I Will Keep You

Safe and Sound

by LORI HASKINS HOURAN

pictures by PETRA BROWN

Scholastic Press · New York

ISBN 978-0-545-19752-6 (hardcover : alk. paper) • [1. Stories in rhyme. 2. Animals—Fiction.] I. Brown, Petra, ill. II. Title. • PZ8.3.H25951w 2013   [E]—
dc23   2011045990 • 10 9 8 7 6 5 4 3 2 1   13 14 15 16 17 • Printed in Malaysia   108 • First edition, March 2013 • The display type was set in Garamond BE. •
The text was set in Adobe Caslon Pro. • The art was created using watercolor, gouache, and brown pencil. • Book design by Chelsea C. Donaldson

For Michael and Jameson,
with all my love

— *L.H.H.*

For Caraid, Elli,
and Callum

— *P.B.*

Brown bears in the den
While the first buds peep

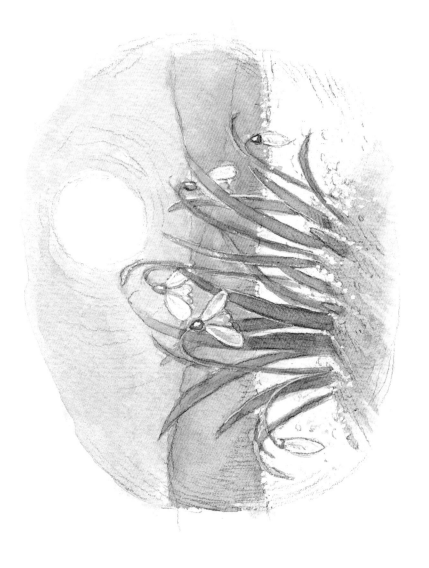

Rabbits in the field

While the crickets cheep

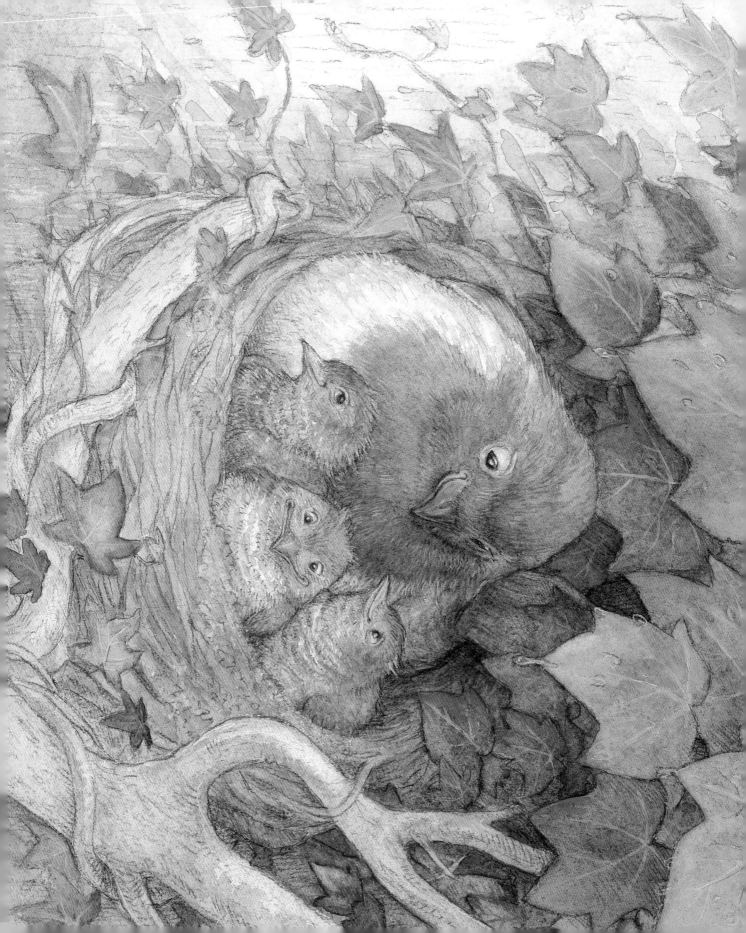

Robins in the nest

While the rain pours down

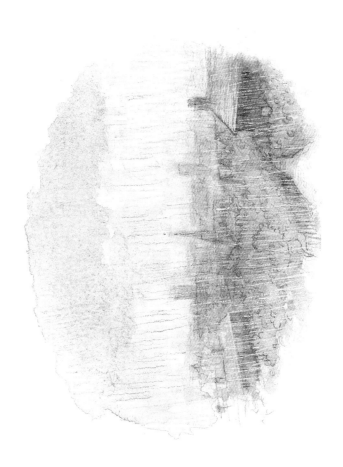

I will keep you safe and sound

Gators in the shade
While the sun burns high

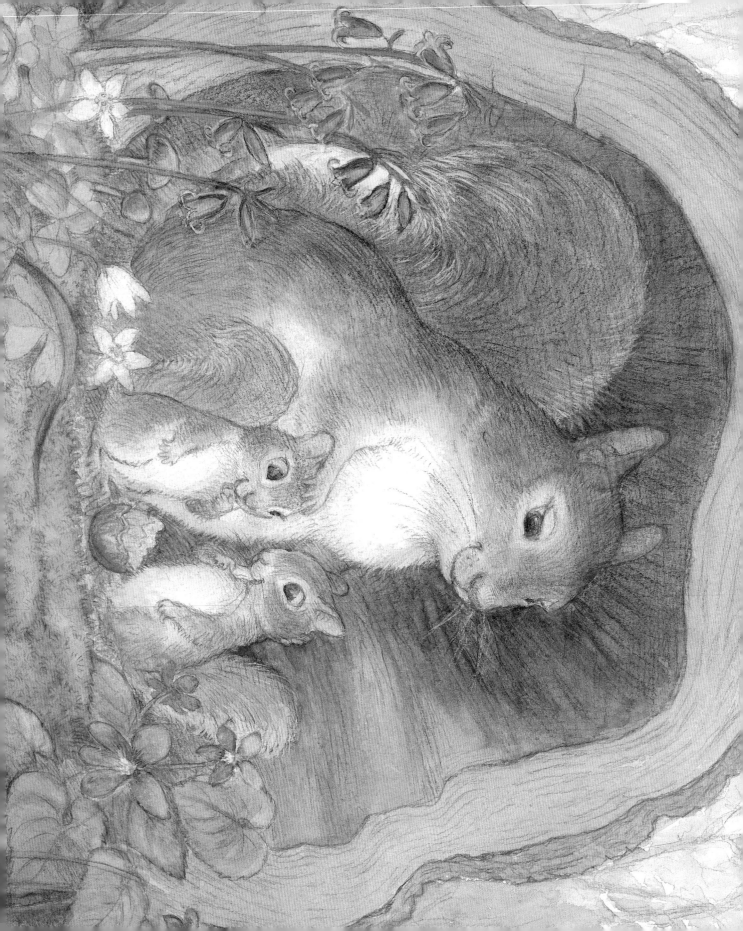

Squirrels in the log
While the hawk sails by

Dolphins in the cove
While the wild waves pound

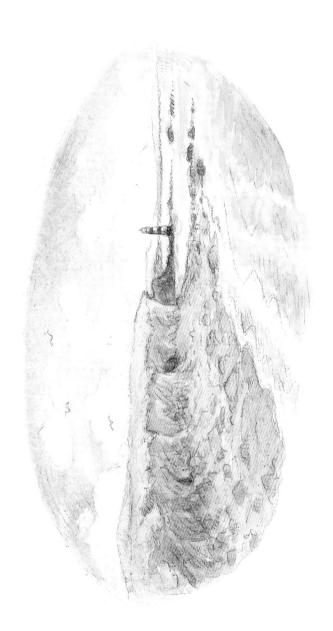

I will keep you safe and sound

Beavers in the lodge
While the strong winds blow

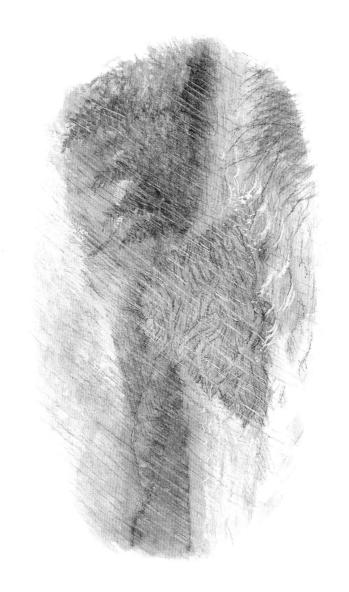

Ponies in the barn
While the sun slips low

Kitten in the moonlight

Lost . . . .

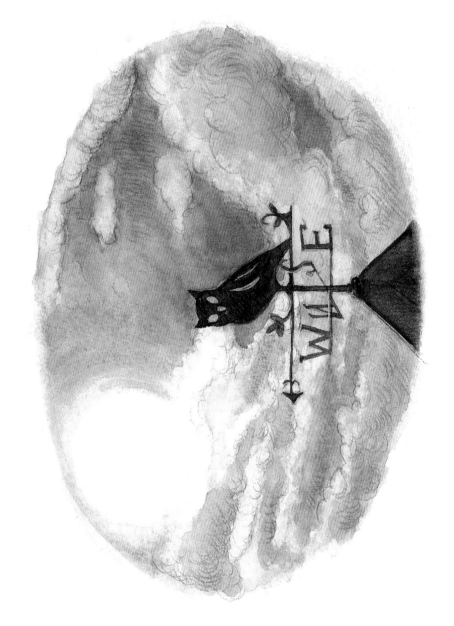

. . . then found

I will keep you safe and sound